Boss Cat

Boss
Cat

by KRISTIN HUNTER

Illustrated by Harold Franklin

Charles Scribner's Sons · New York

for Jacob Mark Sall
in memory of his grandfather
Dr. Manuel Sall

When Tyrone's daddy came home from work Tuesday night, he was singing an Otis Redding tune—and bopping it, too, just like Miles Davis.

Doodle-ee, doodle-oo, bippety BOP boo.

Tyrone could hear his father as soon as he came in the front door. That proved Tyrone had good ears, because the Tanners lived on the fourth floor of the Benign Neglect Apartments, in four rooms plus a kitchen and a piece of roof.

Tyrone ran to meet his daddy coming up the stairs. John Henry Tanner's big brown arms were full of bundles. In one arm, along with the latest issues of *Bronze Talk* and *Black Ballyhoo,* he carried a red plastic tray and a big brown paper bag. Cradled in the other was a cloth bundle that wiggled, with a long black furry thing that looked like a big caterpillar sticking out. The caterpillar-like thing moved from side to side, and the bundle made a faint noise.

Mowr, mowr.

"What you got there, Daddy?" Tyrone asked.

"First let me in the house, boy, and then maybe I'll show you," said John Henry Tanner, huffing and puffing from the hard work of climbing four flights of stairs.

"What you bring us to eat, Daddy?" asked the twins, Puddin' and Dumplin'. Their real names were Clarisse and Charmaine but everybody called them Puddin' and Dumplin'. They were five years old and as big as houses because they never stopped eating. Right now Puddin' had a Mary Jane in her jaw and Dumplin' had a fist full of Ritz Crackers.

"That's what I'd like to know," said Mom from the kitchen. " 'Cause there ain't nothin' in this house but rice and turnip greens and one onion." Mom was slim and pretty, but she was very interested in food too, mainly because she had to cook it.

"I brought catfish," said Tyrone's daddy, pulling a newspaper-wrapped bundle out of the paper bag.

"Oh, goody!" cried Puddin'.

"I love catfish better than *anything!*" cried Dumplin'. When the truth was, she and Puddin' also loved

> beans
> steak
> peas
> turnips
> chicken
> rice
> pigs' feet

(2)

        potato chips
        ice cream
        Alaga syrup
and anything else to eat, just as much.

    The twins made happy noises and crowded around
their father as he unwrapped the package of fish.
They would have made happy noises over any kind
of food.

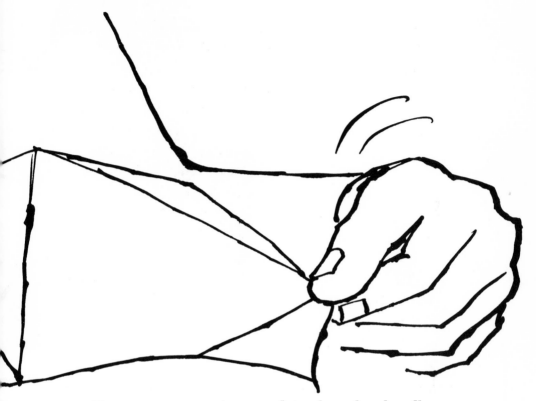

Tyrone was more interested in the other bundle, the one that wiggled.

"What's in there, Daddy?" he asked.

"Open it," his father said.

Tyrone did. He unwrapped the cloth very carefully, and there in the middle of the white bundle was the smallest, blackest kitten he had ever seen. He didn't have one white hair, not even on his belly, and his long black tail was longer than the rest of him.

"Down Home in Georgia," Daddy began in his faraway remembering voice, "we had three cats and four dogs. Plus chickens, goats, cows, bulls, pigs, rabbits, turtles, coons, snakes, sheeps, and alligators."

The twins loved to hear Daddy talk about Down Home in Georgia because there was always plenty to eat there. Watermelons growing in the front yard and corn and collards growing out back. Sugar cane growing everywhere to suck instead of candy. Blueberries, blackberries, raspberries, grapes. Plus peach trees, pecan trees, apple trees, and plum trees. When Daddy talked about all that food, their mouths would water and their tongues would show and their eyes would bug out with wishing.

But Tyrone loved to hear about the wild things Down Home. Slimy swamps and dark woods and spooky cemeteries. Hunting trips and fishing trips in dark, dangerous places. Spooks and spirits and demons and witches. Wild boar, alligators, buzzards, wildcats, panthers, snakes, bears. When Daddy talked about the wild things Down Home, Tyrone would get a good scary feeling. His skin would break out in goose bumps all over, and he would shiver.

"Real alligators, Daddy?" Tyrone asked.

"Yep," said John Henry Tanner. "In the swamp, the Okefenokee. Course we didn't exactly keep 'gators as pets. But I wrestled them once or twice, and I kind of got used to having all kinds of animals around. Our animals were always working animals. The cats caught rats and mice. They were named Fred, Tom, and Sam. The dogs were hunting hounds. They were named Eenie, Meenie, Minie, and Jack, 'cause we wasn't gonna have no Moe."

Tyrone's daddy laughed hugely at his own joke, slapping his leg. The noise scared the kitten, and he ran up John Henry Tanner's pants leg, across his lap, and up his arm to his shoulder. Then he jumped to the floor and disappeared into the kitchen, going a hundred twenty miles an hour, faster than Daddy's Oldsmobile.

Then they all heard a scream.

Oh-oh.

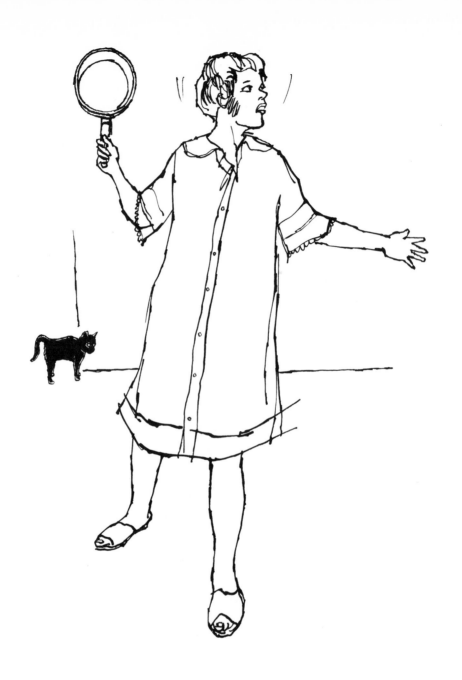

Mom came in with a pot in her hand. "John Henry Tanner," she said, "I was standin' at the stove, stirrin' the rice, when something came flyin' in, ran up my leg, and tore my stocking. I knocked it off me, and it ran and hid under the sink. What kind of devil have you brought home?"

"I just finished tellin' these younguns," Tyrone's daddy said, "about all the animals we used to have when I was a boy Down Home. I figure up here we can at least have us a little bitty old cat."

"John Henry Tanner, you must be losing your mind," Mom said. "Don't you know we have to feed that cat? And clean up after it?"

"Cats look after themselves," Daddy said. "That cat won't be no more trouble than white on rice."

"You mean black on coal, don't you, Daddy?" Tyrone said, making a joke of his own.

Mom didn't laugh. Her eyes got narrow and slanty, like she didn't trust anybody, not even her own husband and children. "What kind of cat is it?" she wanted to know. "Is it Persian or Siamese?"

Tyrone hoped his father would say "Yes" to one or the other, because his mother loved foreign things. She had a twelve-year-old English tweed coat full of moth holes that she wouldn't throw away for anybody. Her favorite food was Italian food. And any hustler on the corner could sell her a bottle of perfume if he told her it was French.

(9)

But Daddy only laughed and said, "What would something Persian or Siamese be doing in *this* house?"

"Is it Abyssinian, then?" Mom asked, her eyes getting even smaller.

"He's a first-rate example of the pure alley breed," said Daddy. "Finest example I ever seen."

"But, Daddy," Tyrone pleaded, "Abyssinian means African. Couldn't he be an *African* cat?"

"Could be," his father admitted. "He might be pure African, at that. 'Cause he sure is pure black."

"Then he's got to go," Mom said. "Black cats are bad luck."

"That kind of talk makes me mad," said Tyrone's daddy. "People like us got no business saying anything is bad 'cause it's black. It's them *other* people who are always talking about

blackball
blackmail
blacklist
black market
black sheep
black-hearted
black lie
and Black Friday.

We ought to know better. The fact is, black cats are *good* luck. And I'll tell you why. The luckiest thing a person can have is a black-cat bone."

(10)

"Then," Mom said, "I'll kill the cat and keep the bone."

At this, Puddin' and Dumplin' both began to cry.

"Shut up, you silly things," Tyrone said to them. "Daddy wouldn't let her do it." But they only cried louder.

From her crib in the big bedroom, Baby Jewel heard them and started crying too. She was the loudest mouth of them all.

"I have heard," Mom said, "that a cat will hang over a baby's crib while she is sleeping and take her breath away."

Tyrone didn't think that was possible. Baby Jewel had more breath than any of them. That was why she could make more noise.

Daddy began singing to himself:
Diddle-ee, diddle-oo, diddy BOP boo.

"I have heard," Mom said, "that looking into a cat's eyes can cause you to go crazy."

Diddle-ee,
Diddle-oo,
Bippity boo.

"I have heard," Mom said, "that a cat's claws are poison and his fur carries germs."

"I think," Dad said, "that I will name him Pharaoh, after the royal kings of Egypt, who were black, just like us."

"Yayyy!" Tyrone cheered, because his daddy wasn't gonna let himself be turned around.

"How you know, John Henry Tanner?" asked Mom.

"I know what I know," said Tyrone's daddy, "because I go to museums and libraries, and read books, and look at pictures, and learn things. I study the *facts.* Not like some superstitious people I know, who only believe what they hear from other ignorant people."

"I am not superstitious," said Mom. "I just don't believe in taking chances. So, since you have brought this demon home, I will just run down to the House of Occult Help and get me some All-Purpose Jinx Removing Spray."

"Waste your money if you must," said Dad, and began singing again.

"Well," said Mom, "if you will kindly remove your black king or emperor or what-is-it from under my sink, I will cook dinner. If I'm not too ignorant to do that."

"When it comes to cooking, you are a professor, my dear," Daddy said. "A Doctor of Potsology."

Mom smiled then. But she wouldn't go near the kitchen till Tyrone went in and got Pharaoh. That was easy because, even though Pharaoh thought he was hiding under the sink, his long, long tail was sticking out. Tyrone laughed and scooped him up.

"You are named," Daddy said to the cat, "for the mightiest rulers in the history of the world, who ruled over the world's mightiest kingdom."

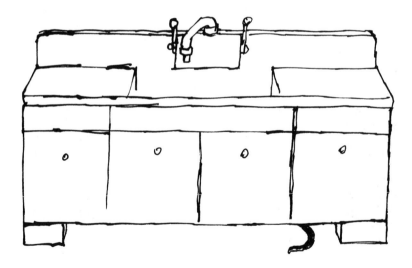

Pharaoh ran away and hid under the stereo, his tail sticking out a mile.

"He don't *act* like no mighty ruler," said Tyrone.

"Give him time," said his father. "He's young right now, but someday he will live up to his heritage. Also, he isn't always scary. He fought me so hard in the car, I had to put him in the trunk to drive him home."

"The landlord don't allow pets in here," Mom said.

"He shouldn't allow *people* in here," Tyrone's father answered. "This building has an advanced case of the falling-down disease. Symptoms are bleeding paint, cracking plaster, hardening of the plumbing, and poor circulation of heat. This apartment house is unfit for human inhabitants."

"Well, why don't we move then?" asked Puddin'.

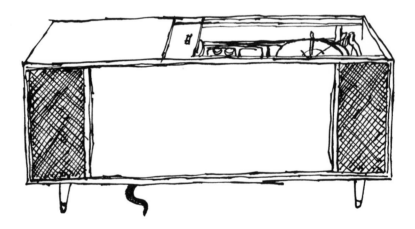

"Because," Dad said, "we are Number One Hundred Ninety on the list for public housing. And one hundred and ninety paydays away from a down payment on a house."

"Well, I do my best," said Mom with a sigh, "hanging curtains and waxing floors and cleaning up after all of you. And if we don't exactly live decent, we at least eat decent. John Henry Tanner, how come you didn't have the heads taken off them fish?"

"I had reasons for leaving them on," Daddy said. "I have reasons for *everything* I do. Look, children. Why do you suppose these fish are called *cat*fish?"

"Because they have whiskers, just like Pharaoh!" cried Tyrone.

"Yes, they look like *cats!*" said Puddin'.

"I hope they don't *taste* like cats. Ugh!" said Dumplin'.

"They taste like *fish,* silly," said Tyrone. "Besides, how do you know what cat tastes like?"

"And that was one reason," explained Daddy. "I am always thinking about these children's education."

"What about their *dinner?*" asked Mom. "I can't cook fish that haven't been cleaned."

"I'll do it, woman!" roared Tyrone's daddy, taking out his pocket knife. "In my lifetime I have caught and cleaned enough fish to be the world's champeen."

"Muhammad Ali's the world's champeen," said Puddin'.

"He's the world's heavy champeen prize fighter," said her father. "But I am the world's heavy champeen fish cleaner. Also corn-shucker, chicken-plucker, apple snatcher and catfish catcher." The way his father made that knife fly, Tyrone believed it. He believed his father could do anything.

"Lot of good it does you, bein' good at those things, livin' in the city," Mom said.

"Too bad for the city," said Daddy, handing her the fish. "It doesn't know what it's missing. Save the heads for Pharaoh. That was my *other* reason."

"Humph," said Mom. And went in the kitchen to cook.

They had a delicious dinner of fried catfish, rice, turnip greens, and pot liquor. Mom was quiet all through the meal, but as soon as the table was cleared, she started up again.

"John Henry Tanner," she said, "we need meat, milk, sheets, shoes, shirts, towels, underwear, and a new kitchen chair. The icebox is fixing to break down for the third time, and I am four weeks behind on my burial insurance. Plus Tyrone's trumpet is in pawn, and your watch, and my engagement ring which never was a real diamond anyway. I tell you all this to say—what do we need with a cat?"

Tyrone thought he would rather have a cat than a trumpet. He couldn't play the trumpet very well anyway.

(16)

"Once in a while," his daddy said, opening a bottle of beer, "it does people good to get something they don't need. You'll get a real diamond on our next anniversary. Or when I hit the number, whichever comes sooner."

Mom's eyes squinted up until they were very, very small. "Who gave you that cat?" she asked. "I know it must have been one of my enemies."

In spite of all her fussing, Mom was happy. That was why she thought she had enemies. Tyrone had heard her say happiness always causes envy, spite, and jealousy.

"The lady who gave me this fine cat," said Daddy, "doesn't even know you. I park her car every day. I take real good care of it, too. And today she said to me, 'Mr. Tanner, remember I told you my Princess had another litter? Well, this is the best one. I know you're a family man, and I want you to take him home to your children.' "

Daddy worked in the garage of the Swankandrank Apartments, where rich people lived. He was a big man there because he could park, drive, wash, and fix any type of car.

"Just one time," Mom said, "I wish them people would give us something we could use. Instead of trouble, aggravation, and an extra mouth to feed and clean up after."

"I tell you, there's no cleaning up after cats," Dad

said, filling the big red plastic tray he had brought home with some stuff that looked like gravel. "This is his bathroom. He already knows how to use it. All you have to do is keep it filled with clean litter. And you don't even have to do that because Tyrone will take care of it. Won't you, Tyrone?"

Tyrone nodded eagerly.

"What's more," Dad continued, "this is a black cat, and we're black folks, so he'll eat whatever we eat. Watch!"

He filled two dishes. Sure enough, Pharaoh ate up all the fish heads and lapped up all the pot liquor. He had better table manners than any of them. He didn't make a sound or spill a drop, and afterward, he cleaned his paws.

"He likes soul music, too," said Tyrone. The long black tail was waving in time to a James Brown record on the radio, and it was right on the beat.

His father poured some beer into another dish. Pharaoh lapped it up greedily.

"And he even drinks Red Cap beer," said Daddy, "which as we all know is preferred by those great black athletes, Hank Mays and Willie Aron."

"You say all that to say what?" asked Mom, watching Pharaoh chase a fly, leap in the air, twist, tumble, and fall in a heap on the floor.

"That it's good to have something black and

beautiful around to remind us to be proud of ourselves."

"Oh, here you come again with that black talk," said Mom. "Black, black, black. Sometimes I think if I let you, you'd hang black curtains at the windows, sleep on black sheets, and cover these walls with black paint."

"Good idea!" said Tyrone. "The dirt wouldn't show."

Oh-oh. What did he ever say *that* for?

"Boy," his mother said, "if you say another word about dirt, I'll make you scrub all this white woodwork in here, even though I already scrubbed it once today. Now, go wash them dishes."

"Awww," said Tyrone, but he obeyed his mother. Pharaoh followed him into the kitchen and wrapped himself around Tyrone's ankles while he stood at the sink. Round and round he went, curling like a ribbon, soft as a furry snake. It felt good. Still, Tyrone thought, he would be glad when Puddin' and Dumplin' were big enough to take turns washing dishes. But that might take forever, since they seemed to grow *out* instead of *up*.

When he finished doing the dishes he went into the living room. Mom, Dad, and the twins were watching *Gunpowder* while Mom gave Baby Jewel her bottle and Dad had another beer. The TV set shook and rattled with the noise of shooting.

Tyrone thought the noise would frighten Pharaoh, but he liked it. He leaped up to the top of the TV set and lay there with his long, long tail hanging down over the screen. The tail waved back and forth so that no one could see the picture.

"Awww!" cried Puddin'.

"Just when it was gettin' good!" said Dumplin'.

"Now we'll never know who shot who," complained Mom.

"Good," said Daddy. He got up and turned the TV

off. "Now maybe we'll get some homework done around here."

"Since when do cats come before people in this house?" asked Mom. "Why should we stop watching TV on account of him?"

"Because," Daddy said, "we watch it too much anyway. I never see anybody open a book around here any more. Do you want these children to become retarded?"

The twins groaned, but Daddy wouldn't turn the

set on again. As for Pharaoh, he lost interest in the TV as soon as it was off. He jumped down and began clawing at the living room drapes.

"Stop that!" Mom cried, stamping her foot. It sent Pharaoh scurrying all the way up to the top of the drapes, where she couldn't reach him. He sat looking down at them with big yellow eyes like Hallowe'en lanterns.

"John Henry Tanner, you see that?" Mom said. "What's gonna happen to my new yellow satin drapes that I'm still paying two twenty-nine a week for?"

"Gangs are on the rise," said Daddy, reading from *Bronze Talk.* "We need better leaders, more playgrounds, more parents and fewer children."

"How we gonna get him down from there, Daddy?" asked Dumplin'.

Her father poured some beer into an ash tray. "This is how." Pharaoh immediately ran down the curtain and came over to drink it.

When he had drunk all the beer, Pharaoh went

over to the big yellow chair, Mom's best chair, the one no one was allowed to sit in because she didn't have plastic slipcovers for it yet. He stood on his hind legs, arched his back, and began scratching at the chair.

Oh-oh.

"What," Mom asked, "is going to happen to my new yellow satin chair that I still owe twenty-three dollars for?"

"I see here," Dad said, turning the pages of *Black Ballyhoo*, "that another preacher was caught stealing from the church Building Fund, and two men shot each other dead in an argument about baseball. On the positive side, the President of Tougaloo College is speaking at the Elks Convention. I think I'll go."

Now Pharaoh was scratching at the rug. Scratch, scratch, scratch. Pretty soon, Tyrone thought, he would make a hole in it.

"What," Mom asked, "is going to happen to our genuine imitation Oriental rug that we still owe forty-four dollars for?"

Dad sang softly.

Doodle-oo, diddy-boo, diddy-roo.

"John Henry Tanner, I'm talking to you!" Mom said. She stuck out her leg. "Look what your cat already did to my stockings. And they're dollar-twenty-nine-a-pair stockings, too, not the cheap kind."

"I'll clip his claws," Dad said calmly. He wrapped

(27)

Pharaoh in an old towel. Letting only one paw stick out at a time, he clipped each claw with a pair of scissors.

But Mom wasn't satisfied. "If you were gonna get something," she said, "you could of got me a big German shepherd dog to frighten off the bad peoples."

"Dogs have no business in the city," Dad told her. "There's too many bow-wows, yip-yips and ruff-ruffs here now, all cooped up in basements and bathrooms and little two-by-four yards. A dog should hunt, not howl. He should run and chase things, else he gets mean and nasty and bites his owner. A cat, now, he don't need much room at all. And he can always keep himself busy."

That certainly seemed to be true. Right now Pharaoh was busy chasing his tail. He didn't seem to know it was attached to him. Round and round he went, till Tyrone got dizzy from watching him.

"Yes," Mom said, "busy tearing up our house."

"And if you're worried about what a *cat* eats," Dad went on as if he hadn't heard her, "you should see a full-grown German shepherd gobble up two pounds of beef a day."

"Mercy," said Mom. "That's more'n *we* eat. But I still don't see what we need a cat for. What *good* is he?"

"What good is Baby Jewel?" asked Tyrone. He was sick and tired of watching his baby sister while

Mom went out to the Wash-A-While or the Market-Rama or the Fire Baptized Holiness Church. All Jewel did was lie on her back and grin silly toothless grins and blow bubbles.

"Don't talk that way about your baby sister, boy," Mom said angrily. "Come get her right now. Take her in and change her and put her to bed. And after that, get busy on your homework."

"Awww," Tyrone grumbled, taking the heavy baby. The moment he hung her over his shoulder, she started crying loud enough to wake up everybody in the Benign Neglect Apartments.

"What did you do to make her cry?" Mom asked, her eyes getting small and squinchy again.

"I didn't do nothin' to her. She's just plain *evil*," said Tyrone. "Why do I always have to look after her anyway?" But he sort of mumbled the words, so his mother wouldn't really hear them.

Oh-oh. What did he do that for?

"If there's one thing I can't stand, it's off-the-wall talk," Mom said. "You may be big for ten, but you ain't too big for me to put 'cross my knee. Come back here and talk straight at me so I can hear you, Tyrone. If you got something to say, that is."

"I ain't got nothing to say," Tyrone said, and carried the baby to her crib, which was in a corner of his parents' bedroom. Pharaoh followed him and rubbed around his ankles like a velvet snake while he plopped

Baby Jewel in her crib and put a bottle in her mouth to keep her quiet. But when he finished changing the baby and tucking her in, he turned around and saw that the kitten was gone.

Tyrone looked all over his parents' bedroom. He looked in his room and the twins' room. He looked under the kitchen sink, under the stove, and under the table. Finally he went back into the living room.

"Daddy, I can't find Pharaoh!" he said.

"He's around here somewhere," said his father without looking up from his newspaper. That was what he always said when he didn't feel like getting up and looking for something: "It's around here somewhere."

"Well, I for one," said Mom, "can't go to sleep with that black cat running loose in this house. He might walk over my face while I'm asleep. Or bring an evil spirit to choke me. Or jump in the crib with Baby Jewel and take her breath away. He might do *anything*. We got to find him."

So Mom and Dad and Puddin' and Dumplin' and Tyrone all started looking for Pharaoh. They looked in all the closets and under all the furniture. They looked behind the drapes and in the kitchen cabinets. They even looked in the icebox and under the rugs.

It was Mom who found him. "John Henry Tanner," she screamed, "this cat is UNDER OUR BED!"

It was true. Pharaoh's long black tail was sticking

out from under a corner of the big bed. It was so dark in the corner that Tyrone hadn't seen it.

"Well, now we know where he wants to sleep," Daddy said calmly.

"Not if I'm alive to do something about it," said Mom. "No cat will sleep under a bed while I am sleeping *on* it. Especially not no *black* cat. It will bring evil spirits that will cause me to have bad dreams. It will give me fits and a heart attack. Since the House of

Occult Help is closed and it is too late to buy a Chase-Em-Away Spray, you will have to put this cat out, John Henry Tanner. Either that, or I go."

"Where will you go?" Dad asked.

"Home to my mother in Ludowici, Georgia. Or to my uncle in Dothan, Alabama. Or to a Divine Heaven nearer by, where no men, children, or demons are allowed, only angels, and I can have some peace and quiet."

Puddin' and Dumplin' began to cry. They would miss Pharaoh, but they would miss their mother, too.

"You just prejudiced against this cat 'cause he's black," Dad said. But he looked unhappy because he knew she meant it.

Tyrone had to do something, so he spoke up. "If you put Pharaoh out, I'll run away from home and join the Snatchandrun gang."

"Ooh, you'll get it when you come back," warned Puddin'.

"I'll never come back, silly," Tyrone told her. "The Snatchandrun gang live in vacant houses. And when they need something to eat or wear, they snatch it and run."

"Stop talking smart, boy," said his father, "and get that cat out from under that bed."

So Tyrone bent down and grabbed Pharaoh's tail and pulled. Pharaoh didn't like that. He dug his claws into the rug to hold on and made loud hissing and spitting noises. It was a tough fight, but Tyrone won because he was stronger.

When he finally got Pharaoh out, he saw why the

little cat had struggled so hard to stay under the bed. He had something to play with, something long and black and silky that looked like another cat. And it was something he knew he had better hide.

Tyrone was so surprised when he saw what it was that he let Pharaoh go. It was the worst possible thing Pharaoh could have found to play with:

> Mom's off-black Semi-Curly Pussy Cat Stretch Wig, for which she was paying five dollars a month by mail.

Oh-oh.

Pharaoh tossed that wig in the air and caught it as it came down.

He grabbed it with his teeth and shook it fiercely.

He batted it halfway across the room with his paw and pounced on it with all four feet.

He snatched it up in his teeth again and ran out of the room.

Pharaoh was really having a good time with that wig. But they all knew it was going to be his last good time in this house. None of them said a word. There was nothing to say.

Daddy went out of the room and came back with the wig. It looked torn-up and raggedy, like alley cat hair. In fact, it looked exactly like another cat Pharaoh had beaten up in a fight. Dad put the wig on the bedside table. Mom wouldn't even look at it.

Dad went out again and got Pharaoh. In a minute

they heard him going out on the roof. He came back with empty hands.

From the roof they could hear a small, sad, lonely cry.

Mowr, mowr, mowr.

"I have a headache," said Mom. "I'm going to bed."

So they all left her in the bedroom with Baby Jewel and went into the living room and sat around.

"Anybody feel like watching television?" Daddy asked. "Bill Cosby is on, also a movie with Frank Silvera."

Though they usually loved to watch anything on TV, and they especially loved Bill Cosby, they all shook their heads. They sat silently for ten minutes, while Dad turned the pages of his newspaper.

Finally Daddy cleared his throat. "A cat can make it anywhere," he said. "He's not dumb and helpless like a dog. He's fast, and he's smart, and he knows how to hunt for food."

Dumplin' began to cry without making any noise. Great round tears rolled silently down her plump cheeks and plopped on the rug.

"You'd be surprised how much food a cat can find down there in that alley," Daddy said.

Puddin' began to cry too. Silently, just like her twin sister.

"Doesn't anybody have any homework to do?" Dad asked.

All three of them shook their heads again.

"He's only a little teeny cat," Puddin' said. "The big cats will eat him up."

"Cats don't eat other cats, silly," Tyrone said. But he was not as sure of that as he sounded.

There was another five minutes of silence. Then Dad said, "Might be some sweet potato pie in the ice box. In fact, I'm pretty sure your mother made a sweet potato pie yesterday."

"I'm not hungry," said Puddin'.

"Me neither," said Dumplin'.

Tyrone knew they *really* had to be feeling bad. It was the first time either of them had said "No" to food.

"Tyrone," his father said, "did I ever tell you about the time my brother and me trapped the wild boar in the south pasture?"

It was Tyrone's favorite story about Down Home. He had heard it maybe a hundred times. But he always said "No" when Dad asked him if he had heard it, so he could hear it again.

This time he said, "Yes."

His father sighed. "Well," he said, "since nobody has any homework to do, and nobody wants to watch television, and nobody's hungry, and nobody wants to hear any stories, I guess I'll say good night."

Tyrone went to his room and undressed and turned out the light. But he lay in the dark without sleeping. When he closed his eyes, all he could see was Pharaoh. Chasing his tail and running up the curtains and hiding under furniture with his tail sticking out. Running through the alley, cold and scared and crying, trying to find food in garbage cans. Hiding from big boys who wanted to throw stones at him and big cats who wanted to eat him up.

He must have been lying there for an hour without sleeping when he heard his mother scream. It woke up Baby Jewel, who started hollering even louder.

All the lights were on in his parents' bedroom. His father was still in bed, but his mother was standing on a chair.

"What's the matter?" Tyrone said.

"There's a THING in here! I think it's a RAT!" cried his mother.

She pointed to the corner.

And there, trembling, scared to move, was a little gray mouse, so tiny that five of him would fit into Tyrone's hand.

"That ain't no rat, it's a mice," Tyrone said.

"Mouse," his father corrected.

"Well, whatever it is, GET IT OUT OF HERE!" Mom yelled.

"I'll set a trap tomorrow," Dad said sleepily, in his it's-around-here-somewhere voice.

"What good will that do me TONIGHT?" Mom wailed. "I won't get a wink of sleep."

"Only one member of this family can catch mice," Dad said, "and he's not here."

"You mean that cat?"

Daddy nodded.

Mom didn't say anything in Pharaoh's favor, but she didn't say anything *against* him either. That was a good sign. Tyrone began to hope a little bit.

Daddy said, "We already lived with plenty of other little critters, such as

     roaches
     ants
     flies
     moths
     gnats
     nits
     chiggers
     chinches
     waterbugs
     and termites."

"I never had bedbugs in my life!" Mom cried.

"These children ain't never had no head lice, neither. And the roaches would be gone from here if the landlord would send the exterminator man 'round regular like he s'posed to. But all he does regular is collect the rent."

She was so angry she jumped down from the chair. But she quickly remembered the mouse and hopped back up again.

"Well, anyway," Dad said, "since we done got used to all them creepy-crawly things, I figure we can get used to a few mice, too. Come back to bed."

But Mom stayed where she was. She took one more look at the mouse and made up her mind. "Bring the cat back in."

"Yayyy!" Tyrone cheered.

"You sure you mean it, Laura Lee Tanner?" Dad asked. "'Cause I don't want to let these children get used to him and then have to put him out again."

"Of course I mean it, John Henry Tanner! That rat is gettin' bigger by the minute! If I weren't so scared to get down off this chair, I'd go outside and get the cat myself! In fact, I think I'll do just that!" She put a toe down toward the floor.

"Oh, no, you won't," Dad said, and she pulled the toe back. "You ain't going outside tonight. The streets ain't safe for women after dark, what with the Snatchandrun gang, the Cutandshoot gang, the Forty Thieves who rob you, the Mau Mau who mug you,

and the Tattoo Artists who cut you up in fancy designs."

"I'd rather face all of 'em than face that rat," she said. But she didn't move from the chair. The mouse didn't move either. Tyrone wondered which of them was more scared.

"Well, only men can go out there at night," Dad said. "Get dressed, Tyrone."

Tyrone dressed in ten seconds, he was so happy. Mom wanted Pharaoh back, and Dad had practically called him a man. Besides, he had never been allowed down in the alley before. Hunting for Pharaoh was going to be the kind of adventure he'd never had with Dad. Like hunting alligators in the Okefenokee.

Pharaoh was not on the roof, so they went down the fire escape. The alley was dark and scary, all right, just like the woods and swamps and graveyards Down Home. There was broken glass underfoot, and lots of

rocks and bottles and other trash, so Tyrone kept stumbling. There were huge hulking shadows, too, and a falling-down piece of wall that something or somebody might be hiding behind, and a vacant house that looked like it might be haunted. Suddenly he was glad he hadn't run away and joined the Snatch-andrun gang. He moved closer to his father.

"You think there might be snakes or alligators down here, Dad?" he whispered.

"Nope, only two-footed animals. But they're the worst kind."

Tyrone knew that was true, because he had watched from the roof and seen them. Bad men and boys like the Forty Thieves hung out in the alley to drink wine, and shoot craps, and fight, and rap, and sing. And he knew that sometimes they did worse things, because he had often seen the cops come to arrest them. Tyrone tried to be brave. He walked ahead of his father.

There was a loud clanging noise behind them, followed by a high spooky yowl and a clatter of gravel. Tyrone jumped and grabbed for his father's hand. Too late. Daddy had turned his back and was shining the flashlight in the direction of the noise.

Then they saw a large, raggedy gray cat with one ear, slinking out of an overturned garbage can.

Tyrone laughed, though his heart was skittering.

"Well," he said, "there's *one* four-footed animal."

"Yes," said Dad, "but it isn't Pharaoh."

They kept searching, but they only had the one flashlight, and every patch of shadow looked like a small black cat—until they turned the flashlight on it and saw that it was a brick or a box or an empty beer can. The alley was full of junk—milk crates, pieces of cars, old mattresses and furniture from people's burnt-up houses—because the City trash men never bothered to clean it. Maybe there were more cats, too. But there was no Pharaoh.

"Guess we better give up, son," John Henry Tanner said. "Guess he's run away."

"I can find him," Tyrone said confidently, in spite of his doubts. He wanted very much to get out of that alley, but he wanted Pharaoh back more.

"Take the flashlight, then."

Tyrone took it and ran toward the darkest part of the alley, which opened into another, wider alley that was really a small street of vacant houses. On his way he stumbled over something round and hard, and the flashlight dropped out of his hand and went out as he fell. He could tell his knees were skinned and probably bleeding, but he did not cry out from the pain. He lay there and felt around in the dark till he found the flashlight lying near the piece of broken pipe that had tripped him. Fortunately it still worked.

Tyrone got up. This time he walked slower, care-

fully shining the light on both sides of the alley. But there was no sign of Pharaoh or of anything else alive.

At the end of the alley his way was blocked by a big black shadow that looked like a dinosaur. Tyrone took a deep breath, then turned the light on it and saw that it was just an old abandoned Buick that some-one had left in the street of empty houses.

"Tyrone, come back here!" Dad called. "You don't know who's sleeping in that car!"

"Wait a minute," Tyrone answered. He crept around the car and finally got up the nerve to shine the light inside. There were no bums or winos in it, but the Forty Thieves had been there, all right. The seats were gone, the steering wheel and radio had been ripped out, and the tires and hub caps were missing, so that the car rested on bare rims of wheels. Flashing the light under the gaping hood, he could see that most of the engine's parts were missing too. Every-thing that people could use had been taken. It was a ghost car that only ghosts could drive. Were there ghosts in the car right now? Or in the vacant houses?

"Boy, do I have to come get you?" John Henry Tanner yelled. He sounded mad.

"Coming!" Tyrone answered, and this time he meant it. It was even quieter than it was dark, quiet enough to scare you if you thought about it. Tyrone was beginning to think about it. He took a step toward his father.

Then he heard the small sound.

    Mowr, mowr.

It was somewhere behind him.

Tyrone turned back and shined the flashlight toward the sound, all over the back of the car. The light fell on a corner of the partly opened trunk. Hanging out of it was a long, long black tail.

"I found him!" Tyrone cried.

"Good work, son," said his father, who only needed to take four big steps to be right beside him.

"He was hiding," Tyrone said, "because he's scary. But he's too dumb to hide very well. He always forgets to hide his tail."

"You know what *I* think happened? I think he felt brave enough to explore, so he got down here all right, but then he got scared and couldn't get back up again. So he crawled in here and found a home."

"Because," Tyrone said eagerly, "he remembered riding in the trunk of *your* car. Maybe Pharaoh's not so dumb after all."

"Cats can go from dumb to smart and from scary to brave, all in a few minutes. Just like boys," said Daddy.

And he put the arm he wasn't using to carry Pharaoh around his son's shoulders.

Diddle-ee,
Diddle-oo,
Bippety BOP boo,

sang Tyrone as they climbed back up the fire escape.

When they got back inside they were greeted by the twins in their pink Size-Eleven-and-a-Half-Chubby nightgowns. Clothes wide enough for them were always too long, and Mom didn't always have time to take the hems up, so the nighties dragged behind them like evening gowns with trains.

"You found Pharaoh!" shrieked Puddin'.

(50)

"Give him here!" cried Dumplin'.

Even though Pharaoh's glossy black fur was covered with dust and dirt from the alley, they took turns holding and petting him till their pink fronts were streaked with gray.

"Tyrone found him," Daddy said. "But don't play with him now. I only keep working animals, and it's time for this one to get to work." He took Pharaoh

into his bedroom and set him down in the corner where
the mouse had been.

"Smell, boy," he said, rubbing Pharaoh's nose
against the baseboard. "Find the hole."

Tyrone could have told without looking that the
mouse had run away, because his mother had come
down from the chair. She was in the living room,
watching a Late Late Late Charlie Chan movie. She
had combed out the funny-looking braids she wore
to bed and under her wig, and she looked calm and
pretty again. But her feet were drawn up under her
to keep from touching the floor.

"I am trying," she said, "not to think about rats and
mice."

"You keep doing that," Daddy said, and sat down
on the sofa beside her, "and just relax because the
men of this house have things all taken care of."

Tyrone felt warm all over with pride. He was one
of the men of the house. So, he supposed, was
Pharaoh.

"Tyrone found Pharaoh!" said Puddin', dragging
her gown behind her into the room.

"Pharaoh's finding mice!" said Dumplin', stepping
on her sister's train.

"Can we stay up and watch TV till he finds them?"
asked Puddin'.

"We can't sleep," Dumplin' explained, "because
we're hungry."

"You can stay up," Mom said with a sigh, "but you can't have anything to eat because I won't touch my feet to that floor to walk to the kitchen. Not as long as there's rats and mice in here."

"They eat too much anyway," Tyrone observed. For once, Mom didn't get mad. And they all sat down to watch the movie.

During the first commercial, Pharaoh came in with something in his jaws and dropped it on the floor in front of Mom.

"Ugh! Ooh!" she cried, and tried to climb up on the back of the sofa.

"It can't hurt you now. It's dead," Tyrone said.

Tyrone's daddy picked up the dead mouse by its tail. "Good boy," he said, scratching Pharaoh's ears. "Now get back to work."

"John Henry Tanner, you think we can go back to bed now?" asked Mom.

"Wait a while," said Dad. "Mice don't live by themselves. When you see one, chances are you've got a whole mouse family in your house."

So they went on watching the movie.

During the second commercial Pharaoh came in with another mouse and dropped it at Mom's feet.

"He's bringing you presents. He likes you," said Puddin'.

"I've had presents I liked better," Mom said. But she didn't say anything more against cats.

"I think he's found the nest," Dad said.

Sure enough, Pharaoh came back during the third commercial with another mouse. And then he brought another. And another.

When "The End" came on the TV screen, they had watched thirty minutes of movie and twenty-five commercials. And Pharaoh had caught five mice.

"Pharaoh's the greatest!" cried Dumplin'.

"He's the world's heavy champeen mouse catcher!" said Puddin'.

"He's a boss cat," said Tyrone. "Every ghetto family should own one."

"You don't own a cat, he owns you," Dad said. "He rules himself and his kingdom. That's why I named him for the mighty kings of Egypt."

And then Pharaoh did something to prove Dad was right. He sat there looking at the TV as if he were about to spring up on top of it and lie there with his tail swinging in front of the screen. But Dad turned the set off, and Pharaoh jumped up on the yellow satin chair instead.

Oh-oh.

They all looked at their mother, expecting her to scream. But Mom didn't say a word. She just smiled.

"Mom, none of us children can sit on that chair," Puddin' complained.

"That's right, you can't," her mother said. "But *Pharaoh* can."

"Cats are cleaner than people anyway," Dad observed. "They take baths all day long."

Sure enough, Pharaoh was taking a bath in the yellow chair. He licked all the alley dust from his fur until he was shining and clean again. Then he sat up proudly and purred.

"Pharaoh is on his golden throne!" cried Tyrone.

"But I'd feel better," Mom said, "if he would come and sleep under my bed again. Just in case that was a *large* mouse family, with more than five children."

She got her wish. As soon as the living room lights were turned off, Pharaoh scurried into the big bedroom and ducked under Mom's side of the bed, leaving his long black tail sticking out.

"Sure makes me feel good to see that," Mom said.

"Ain't you scared of witches and nightmares?" Dad teased.

"I'm much more afraid of rats and mice," she answered.

And after they had said good night and turned out their lights Tyrone heard her say,

"I guess maybe black *is* beautiful. At least when it comes to cats and people. I don't much care for it in furniture, though,"

and,

"I never liked that wig much anyway. I'm going to get a new one,"

and,

"Wait till I tell my friends that we have a real Egyptian cat!"

And,

"John Henry Tanner, when you pick up something for dinner, you be sure and get something nice for that cat. You hear?"

Tyrone's father only snored.

But Tyrone knew he would do what she said.

Because Pharaoh was now the mighty ruler of their kingdom.

DATE DUE

10-14			
OC 05 88			
WITHDRAWN FROM			
OHIO NORTHERN			
UNIVERSITY LIBRARY			
GAYLORD			PRINTED IN U.S.A.